The Mind Is Mighty

This Book Is Dedicated to…

Everyone I've ever known for their strength,
and for expressing the reality of their lives.
For the effort, they put into understanding
and empathising with the lives of others

It is my view that their strength plays a huge part
In ending the stigma attached to Mental Health
And those who struggle

About This Book:

This book is for anyone who is interested in Mental Health.
I've chosen to write from the view of several people, and to my best ability, pay attention to *how* it has affected people I've met and people I've known through the years.
My journey has begun in the 1980's, right through to the present day.
Sadly, as so many of us will now be aware, people with various struggles with their Mental Health, are still being misunderstood and may continue to be alienated.
There is simply no need for this lack of understanding to continue. No one is entirely exempt from the possibility that their own Mental Health could suffer at any given time

I have and still do suffer with my own struggles and demons
But in this book I've referred to someone in the first person, although that someone isn't necessarily me and I have decided to do it this way, in order to express various
Situations. Therefore, I refer to '*I, he and she*' all for the same reason

Thank you for your interest

Alys

Table Of Contents:

Table Of Contents: continued

Phrases:

Hell Knows

I see real people,
I see tired eyes
Real grumbles, real smiles -
And in such anguish,
I've laughed, I've cried
But was I real?
Hell knows, I tried.

I heard real people
Real lives
Unreal dreams,
behind those eyes
Often anguish,
would torment and pry...

...And cling to them,
not letting go --
Not letting love -
move me,
so slow --

Real people,
I see real lives
Heard quiet fear, on clear nights
I took those steps,
to face those heights
But was I real?
Hell knows... I tried

Stigma is outdated
Stigma, contaminated…
Stigma is cruel
It's as polluted as the fuel in the air
I'm uncomfortable with stigma

There Were No Words

If I *speak* a cliché, it's because I'm undone
I'm no complete item,
nor an unfinished gift,
not even a purchase, waiting to come.
If you *hear* my cliché, it was the best I could do
Will you love me so real, for a moment or two?

If I repeat my cliché,
if I reveal who I am,
will you step inside… my turbulent mind,
if you can?
I am not ready to be...
a gift or a treasure
and I've an unhealthy fear within all my pleasure
I frown at my cliché, but what else could I say?
For I need you beside me, with a touch of midday

If I fly, if I run
If my words come undone
I may banish my cliché, and head for the sun
Fill a life-long ambition as you sing me to sleep
And become a new item, with a belonging complete.

The Silence That Comes

You are so hurt, you've become silent
You've remain silent - the hurt has stepped in
Your lack of energy, is like that of a lifeless being –
And all because the hurt -
silenced everything, yet again

So much hurt is beyond comprehension –
to people who have hurt you, themselves
You tell yourself that you have no purpose –
And you silence everything else

Silence is like a fistful of words,
that have been bagged and unable to burst
And you deny yourself –
A sense of *self worth*

Was I Dying In My Mind?

I may never know why,
one minute I fly
And the next, I feel dead,
but without
wanting to die.

I always see life,
when I rise with the highs
But when I sink, am I dying?
Am I dying in my mind?

I may never know why,
the world deceives my eyes
I feel I'm leaving all I'm here for,
Am I living in disguise?

The more I know about myself,
the more sense I am to *me*
But I still don't know, if I was flying, flying.
Or was I dying in my mind?

**Do all you can to like what you see
in the mirror
It's not all about *'features'*
It's all about self belief
It's all about who you are and who you can become**

I Won't Face You

Mirror deceiver -
you owe me so much
You show me so much of myself
It would be so much better
if you were covered with dust -
Or facing the wall, on a shelf

Mirror, who made you,
for all you are is a frame
I was okay til I looked,
until you got in my way
I am tempted to move you,
another place, another wall
Or facing the window --
and I won't *face* you at all

I will buy me some flowers,
leaves and long stems
And all made from cotton,
they can gaze at themselves
See reflections of fabric,
through the glass of the frame
As for me --
I will never be looking again

The Anonymous Teen (part one)

He was empty, so he climbed to the top
With no doubts at all, he found places to stop
He was numb above town
Just a someone looking down
I felt his numbness tightening,
And I... am thinking now

What will he do? Will he let himself go?
Or will he descend…
with footsteps...
slow?

...and back down to town, below all that he climbed
where he daren't look at life, with his half opened eyes
Unwanted noise, and enlarged in his mind
Stability breaking, like the half severed ties

He thinks of a tightrope, he stays at the top,
where the tower is engaging with the depth of the drop
He thinks of a circus, and what acrobats do
His numbness grows weaker,
but what did he do?
Did he let himself go?
And who do I speak of...and who did he know?

I'm thinking now, I still see his scar
I still know of demons who were never that far...
from scenarios of trouble,
and from lingering hate

...And who do I speak ok?
And was it too late?

The Anonymous Teen (part two)

Let me take a piece of your darkness,
one step, and you'll be free
Don't head towards the tunnel on your own
Or on the road, or the edge of the field
Let me take a moment to listen
One word is all I need
Let them do what they feel they need to
Let them bathe those cuts on your feet
A shroud of sadness surrounds your life
And I know you are still shaking and so weak
Let me take a piece of your darkness
Let us take the driving seat

And then we'll head for that city field
And then we'll talk about those streets
But just for now,
let me take that shroud
Let them bathe your blood cut feet

(The anonymous teen (part two only)
Based on an experience of meeting a young man
in the 1980's, who was in his late teens
The details have been purposely been left vague)

The coiled spring of anxiety
The burden of exhaustion

Can You See Me?

A stone bridge above me
And barriers beside me
Chains all around me.

Weighing me down.

Trying to get off
the old railway line
The rattling of chains
from a local tin mine
No one above me
No love beside me
Just the iron around me.

 Weighing me down.

I try to get out
of my tormented mind
But the voice in my head
Is just trouble I find
No water below me
And under this bridge,
too many barriers
that simply won't give
No lock to unfasten
my desperate plea
Just fear of something,
or someone,
….or me

Getting Weaker

She was sleeping soundly, and had been for some time
She was curled up on a hospital chair

Starvation --

She only ate salad, no salad cream.
No milk or sugar in coffee or tea.

Prison or hospital? --

No care for her illness, although that's why she was there.
Frail, exhausted...
unable to bear,
the treatment so cold
And what a wonder she is...
And will her story be told?

Desperation --

Often, she hears the trolley arriving, smells the meals
getting close to the ward
She gets up and leaves,
But she's dragged back again, by the arm...
and through a long corridor.

Force-fed --

They push her, but this time, it's onto the chair
They force food to her mouth
Anguish,
despair
Her tears that mingle with the food as it falls...
You could hear the whole room,
scream through the walls.

More or less, left to die --

Staff losing patience, with a lady this ill...
But no need to worry...
they can now force a pill...
        Into her system,
        into her mind
They never knew Carol...
but if they had tried...
for it wasn't impossible...
She was easy to find.

*(A tribute to a young woman I met and talked with
about her battle with an eating disorder in the UK
during the 1980's.
She was in her late twenties at the time
and she has stayed in my mind ever since)*

**Prewritten labels hanging on hooks
Boxes to tick
One large text book…**

For better…For worse

Being Alone

He makes no eye contact
He's often withdrawn
He is quiet, but there is more –
With his eyes closed tight – there was a world to explore

He'll find company there
He'll be on the outside - On the edge of a circle --
But there are days when he tries --
To be *part of* the circle –
for it's lonely out there –
On the outside, where the billboards are bare

He was an innocent youth, but now he smiles like a man
Fulfilling his dreams - *if he can*
He still stands on the outside – where his circle was formed
Exchanges the smiles, as he paints on street walls
He creates such an image of what it is like –
To be alone on the outside –
But to value his life

He *rarely* makes contact with the wide world outside
He's a beautiful loner, and I'm sharing his pride

It Was Light Before I Was Ready

Awake in the zombie hours
In a moon-filled room, some shade of blue –
that devours my sense of myself

Awake, awake for too many hours
I stare at the mess on the shelf

The hidden clock behind handkerchiefs,
nail polish, books and 'things'
Some squinting I do, as I turn myself round
And away from the shelf –
And the bluest of blue

Out of the blue, out of the blue –
I shudder as my thoughts are devoured
Only one hand ticking, I see in my head –
What am I doing? Am I a coward?

I'm ticking on one hand, I'm still on the next,
for too many hours, and for a night left unsaid

Awake, awake!
Awake in the moon
In the zombie-like hours, in some shade of blue
What did I see, and did I turn to you?
What kind of person did *I* turn into?
I am now taken, back to the time,
where everything happened but where *sleeping dogs lie*
The clock remains hidden –
and with no sense of *me*
I remember the trauma, that maybe, could be,
The cause of these hours where sleep eludes me

As awake as I am, I block out the moon,
too blue and uncanny, and too much like the doom
With no sense of *me,* I need to scribble away,
On tattered blank paper –
And wait –
wait for the day
No sleep! *No sleep for the wicked,* my grandma would
say
Is that why I lie here?
Did I find you there?
Lying with sleeping dogs
And did we care,
did we care?

I've a feeling I'm crazy - it came out of the blue
I'm desperate for sleep - so where is the moon?

You deserve to experience pleasure
You just don't *feel* you deserve to experience it

Thou Shalt Not

The potatoes are still warm, and the biscuits not quite
soft
And all the time she lives this way, you tell her

Thou shalt not!

So she takes herself to where there is no pleasure,
To where there is no rest
She walks around the town each day,
Always tries to look her best
Screaming through her silent lips,
And bitten by regret

Into the food, she *has* got this,
And she feels it's all she's got
What *they* don't know…
But what they say, is…

Thou shalt, Thou shalt not!

The screaming mind, the weakened ways
The grip it has, those every days
The food she'll eat, the food she'll hide
And all the time, the bite inside…
The hungry heart, the hollow eyes,
The yelling help from those who tried…
They got it wrong,
Or they did not care
They focused on her body bare
But alive, and all for what?

Don't go there… For Thou shalt not!

Cryptic Meanings

These thoughts are etched onto my forehead
I'm sure they weave into my mind
Every cryptic meaning getting silent...
in the crevice it will find

Ahead of me, I see reflections
And recollections call
They pull me into deeper darkness,
...this is where I fall

This is where I block it out, where I stop and where I
lie...
silently upon the bed, but *never*, will I cry

Trauma cannot seize my tears
...this is where I fail
Is fail a word I should not choose?
I'll say it anyway
There it was, the darkness... dark, and the pain my
forehead feels
Recollections that call on me, are making this too real

I jumble things together, I endure every mess
For details shall elude me soon, but will they lie to rest?

My mind repeats in panic mode
I've not yet blocked it out… or found a different focus...
I hear my mother shout
I hear my father at the gate
I hear the barking dog
I saw a shadow through my window,
But I had no time to wait

I'm sure these thoughts are etched forever, upon my forehead
sore
And I still remember rushing home while she waited at the
door

I mix a potion in my mind, it may just help me sleep
And now I lie upon my bed, but never will I weep

Thoughts are etched onto my forehead
They are vivid to my mind
I feel them creeping, sure but silent...
in the crevices they find

My mother hears me,
My father leaves
My dog, he bears his teeth
I saw a figure through my window
It was you...
in disbelief

Demons need me
Maybe I need them;
After all,
they did paint some awesome patterns on my wall

There's A Pattern To This

Demons chase your mind. Don't let them take it
Don't let them run away with you. *Just don't run*

Ease yourself away --
In your own time --
at your own pace
Just don't let them chase

Yes, you want to get away -- so you *will* want to run
You *will* put your head in your hands - as they come --

You want them out - and you want to push them aside
Don't battle with demons - they are up for a fight!

All this sounds easy - but none of it is
And everyone's different - there's a pattern to this --

Take yourself somewhere. Out or indoors
Within the strength of yourself -- You *can* explore

Let demons ride - they will tire for sure
Can you accept them?
Let them fight their own war?

They exhaust you, I know --
And none of this is --
And everyone's different --

But in your pain --
you still *live*

Adrenaline

It may have been a crazy thought
It was like an accidental pattern.
A flow of the past, came to the fore
I find it hard, to block out what happened

The flow dispersed, I felt it may leave me
I needed that knowledge… that sense of belief
But where would it go?
And *go* for how long?
All that flows deeply…
will flow on…
flow on…

…The past, it can switch itself on,
And go on…
And inside the struggle is a need to belong
A need to be certain
A need to be **you**
Accidents happen…
And thoughts *always* do

You may have been crazy…whatever that means
And mostly know nightmares,
And rarely know dreams
You *need* a belief, and you need it to stay…
For life is just crazy, and we **all** need a way

I long for my diary… my thoughts kept on rushing
Melancholy visions,
Then mayhem like *something*…

Something, I'm not sure, for the past is my blur
I try to erase it, but my mind is too clear

I see through the darkness that chill in the air
When I was a teenager who was there…
Nervously *there*!

My words are now bleeding, in my diary, I write,
about more of what happened, on those cold winter
nights

In shock…
Stunned…
No sense of time
A life lost to suicide,
The most broken of minds

This Feeling Has A Name

I'm in the bubble, I walked straight inside
I still saw the world around me, but I was otherwise occupied
I have a name for this old feeling
Although it's meaning - I can't explain
When a solitary raindrop came without its rain
It invited me to step inside, a bubble as it were
All was still for one deep moment, apart from one small bird
A sparrow sitting, flapping, chirping, in the gutter to the eaves
It was not to far above me, well that's what I believe
Clothing on the washing line, blew softly I am sure
Everything is now slow motion, everything and more
In a trance I may have been, I'd lost all sense of time
From the bubble, I focus on a world --
not yours - and certainly not mine
Was I a bearer of some bad news?
Did I create this bubble shape?
With so much room to move around, I've no desire to escape
T shirts, jeans, socks and shorts - they slowly, barely move
I think it's getting close to dark,
Is it time we ate some food?
Do I step outside my bubble?
Shall I wait for you to speak?
Dare I touch the world outside --
In my bubble warm but bleak?

A Cherry On A Cake

The cake. Tempting you to take -
a sugar sweet, soft to touch
Too nice to eat...but too nice to not!
The smell of what was baked

A bite to take, smoothly sliced
But wait!
The guilt - the pleasure?
Guilty -- pleasure
Wait!
One mouthful. One more. One more
Too many -- and then no more!

The cherry on the top
The look of every drop of jam
Cherry dome -- secret eating,
from your home
The secret eat, Sacred 'treat'?
Don't knock her door, don't call
She could not answer – all she sees is cherry small

Glisten - The cherry that tops the icing thin
So skilled, are you
at under-slicing --
Agonising - you cannot win!
The cake. And the guilt, that eats away at you

One sweet morsel. A frenzy follows
Guilt
Shame - Into a tomorrow
You only have yourself to blame?
No!
For all just eats away at you --
One bite,
One bite
One bite, then two

The cake. A *perfect, perfect* bake --
since when!?
Your thoughts consume you - yet again

The cake
The lightest touch
You are -- the lightest touch
You could not stop
It's too late now -
and just too much

A constant battle
All alone
Secret eating from your home
The shame you feel
The cherry glaze
Tasting lush
And now you crave - to lose the day

You pay the price - torment and shame

The secret slice - was baked for pain

I try not to allow anyone
to tell me how I should be thinking…
There isn't always a *right* way,
And there isn't always a *wrong* way…

But there is your own *unique* way

We May Never Know

Are we ill?
Are we well?
Is it all about our health?
We are young and we are old
Are we crushed?
Are we content?
Do we avoid all that we've felt?
Are we really understood?
Are we ready and is all good?
Are we ill?
Are we well?
Do we really have to tell?

I can speak out -
loud and proud
But are we really understood?
We are human after all
And as ourselves –
we need to fall
Will we struggle?
Will we sleep?
Our bodies fail to speak
We do this --
And we do that --
And after all -
Life can be late – in teaching us so much --
About the damage and the pain
And in the light of all we learn –
We still find, we can't explain

No Hesitation

The suicidal thoughts
You can't distract yourself -
not at that very moment in time
In that moment, you **are** in those thoughts
These thoughts go through a process, and **they** are on form
Without hesitation, **you** install them all

Some will fall asleep – others can't
Some will speak – others can't

Head space – what you may be thinking about
Like someone in a tunnel
Someone trapped
Only you yourself could maybe work this out –
But when? For there is a need to be distracted
But this is so hard to do yourself

Looking into a tunnel.
Tunnel vision – you can't see a way –
you can't see an alternative

Trapped.
There is a sense of entrapment

The Questions And Request

Today I can't relate to anyone
Talk? No, it's not a possiblity
Listen? Yes okay, but I'll be miles away
Grateful? Yes I am, for everything I have
Guilty? Yes, of not being able to show the gratitude I feel

I see the clifftop sturdy, whilst all around it moves
Each blade of grass, and brittle stone and the clothing that I
wear
I feel I am an error...
I feel I may just never...find my way
Today I've no idea which way I'll go. Today I can't relate
There are no dreams, just destinies, and I've words I'd like to
say
But who would want to hear them,
so...within my head they'll stay

Today I can't relate to anyone, I'm many miles away
Upon a clifftop sturdy...
Where all around it moves
I pull my ragged sleeves, over blistered hands
I'm waiting for my destiny, it's wish is my command

All around me shows its rhythm
I see the globe, I see myself...
I listen to the waves a beating
Please don't feel guilty...
when I am dead

Five Weeks

The tunnel of nothing but pale green walls.
The letting go of solid wooden doors

They were left to slam.

While the lack of voices echo.

You took from her, what she came here with.
And you cared not... for who she wept for.
She, with all her warmth...
some say....was left to suffer.

And some may say, you did your job
You cared not...
but simply watched her.

And heard the words as no great value

Just the doors, let go, then slam

You divided them,
and all their knowledge...
Those two friends, who laughed a little,
and curled up together
when you were not around.

You neglected her companion
And dragged her to her bed.
Removed all of her belongings...

Then you told her...
she was dead.

And that was it!

That was it, and yes you really knew...

That she would be bewildered, while no comfort came
from you

It is this hollow...
empty,
echoing,
that she still can never bear.
For in the corridor of green,
her voice became aware

One echo in the chamber,
of sparsely painted walls.
One loss, that covered up her name,
that you never chose to call

And this was how the pale green echoed...
through doors and solid walls

Let go!
And slam... The separation that
that no medicine could bind
Letting go
but haunted still...
And no cure for her mind.

(*My words as a tribute to a friend whom
          I still miss dearly*)

Not haunted in a sense
Just haunted by events
Needing what will hurt us…
For sometimes,
it's important that we *never* will *forget*

I Want To Go Back

It's been an ancient year and I didn't invite the ghost
to stroke my hair
So I haven't felt the comfort on my scalp
And now, I just want to go back –
simply to *be* there

It's been an uneasy morn, and there's a ghost who stays
in my heart
I want him to be there, but at the same time –
I'm *torn*
I want the comfort of an embrace
I want to *remain* - withdrawn
His nails, I hear them –
on the flakey painted door –

And you peep inside the room
My ghost had begun another life,
…Methodical and New

My ghost had listened intently to my request
He left my heart no more
but in its restful focus,
I was obviously Torn

And in everything I do, my perception - fragile,
talks to *you*
I listen to another life –
and ghosting what I do -
I am the mother to a newly born
And in restful focus,
My heart is *Torn*

The perfectionist
She said she felt like kicking herself
for she was *never good enough*

Too unfamiliar

She was *unfamiliar* with positivity
Too tuned-in, to familiarity
And always replaying the *harshness* of reality

She could still feel the words
that were stronger than hers
They were louder and puffed up with pride
The misconception that *those* words were wise

Too unfamiliar with positivity --
Too tuned-in, to familiarity --
She'd been *replaying the past* for too long

*"You've done all that girl - You've been there before
sweetheart, you've been pulling at your flaws* for so long
—
That it's simply time to let go

All Those Things

I've survived the madness
It will linger no more
I survived the dread -
and I will take the fore

I have held the nightmares -
the fictive flow,
I recognise them -
I just about let go

I survived starvation
It shall never come again
And I took the insults -
I took my shame to hell

I have held my loved ones -
the real hearts
And I will travel weightless -
to be where they are

I have planned for the worst,
and hoped for the best
I have felt myself dying -
(Very few know the rest)
I have recognised trauma -
the hold, the control
I will find myself - always
And I will not let me

Lost For No Reason

You've cared for someone
many times -
maybe more than I have
And lost yourself far too often -
and lost yourself - for what?
Hurt, it hounds you -
and pain, peruses you -
You've felt *all this* -
for what?

You've given love
so many times -
Too many times to mention
You lose it - plunge into the pain
because you found that *someone*

You put up your guard -
then left it there
But love, is *so much* stronger
You feel the reasons to let love in -
And for that you will -
surrender!

You slip - but find yourself –
So many times -
With or without love --
With or without emptiness --
And with or without doubt

And in-between the hurt and pain,
you work your own self out

Caught up with life,
and what life can do
And with what life has done
And how so many things…

Could destroy you

Endlessly

Gambling - lost everything
Drinking, still lost
Addicted - you're fighting
You gamble... but at what cost!?
Starvation - you're wasting
Binging, your pain
Compulsive - the cycle
It's written in pain
Depression - the empty
Bipolar aware
Anxiety that tires you
Then repeats - with no care
Voices that call you
Lost are the days ---
When obsession will strike you
Again,
and again
Abuse - in the nightmares
Neglect and self worth
Drinking, eating, the drugs of this world
Psychosis - the chaos
You cannot sleep --- cannot leave
Lost are the years –
(We are conscious of grief)
Trembling - the symptoms
The 'side effect' trap
Repeat --- repeat – Is there ever a gap?
Is there ever a space?
Some place for the mind
You will get yourself back –
And the people who care –
will know ... that you tried

Inner Voice

You have a persistent voice that challenges you all the
way
Challenges you… to think the worst.
But it's natural for the inner voice to be with you…
And to complain…
Especially when you're in the midst,
and so completely sensitized.

Logic can be missing...
so these obstructive thoughts, are simply
human thoughts
and quite '*normal*' if you like.

Hear them...listen
Listen to,
the inner you…
Listen to it all...but don't allow them,
to *over-power* you.

When they begin to beckon...
Let them happen…
For *you* are only being challenged once again.

This challenge may be the only way to find yourself,
and when you do…
You can become detached
And with this,
you can move on… to eventually find **you**

It may seem like an enormous task,
but in reality, it can be done.

Remove yourself, to a certain extent,
then rise above it all.

And finally, *listen*... yes!
But deny the voice that controls you
with it's call.

A list of phobias could never complete
She searched the lives
of people wanting to talk…
of fear, and why…
fear can intensify

When Nothing Is Without Fear

I fear noise. You fear crowds
He fears being looked at. She fears being out
I fear illness. You fear dogs
He fears buttons. She is fearful of inhaling smog

I fear breaking things. You fear time
He fears many things. She fears crime
I fear losing someone. You fear food
He fears contamination. She fears her own mood

They live in fear. We are misunderstood
We try to hide the broken water
We'd escape this if we could
You may not look at buttons
You may never be alone
There are some things we can go without
Are you safe while you are home?

The Rag Doll

Her spirit yearned, and she always tried...
But she always stood on the edge - the outside
Hair tied up in bobbles jade…

…She was never tailor made

She wasn't cut out… in any particular way
She wasn't stitched or neatly shaped
She held herself upright, but lost her way…

…She was never tailor made

With timid smiles and withdrawn eyes
She was barely audible, pale and shy
Like a handmade doll, in worn-out play…

…She was never tailor made

Just like the doll, that flopped and shone,
with feet and fingers neat
She sat upon the window ledge,
And looked out on the street
She was a whisper worthy of love
with stitching crimson
In a world above…

… that was never tailor made

Feeling Persecuted

With closed eyes, she curled up tightly, then pulled her
knees towards her chin -
And then she wept
With curtains closed, she consoled herself, with the
photographs she'd kept
In peachy fragrant light, she simply told herself -
they are photographs, and nothing else
But still, she wept

Her fingers, they were aching -
Tightly, tightly she was gripping - gripping onto herself
Barely weeping, barely waiting -
for her life to reappear -
Oh how she dreamed of being –
Someone else ---
Anyone, but herself

The shadow lurking over her, was that of her own flesh
A shadow with a beating heart, a shadow of herself
Fingers aching, eyes sore and red –
She looked at photographs
They were real, and in her mind –
They were shadows of herself
Uncurl the fingers, unravel all,
The woven mapped out lives -
that on sealed lips, would dare not utter --
What *you should dare not* find

It doesn't necessarily matter
what other people think of you,
but it can still damn hurt
There are certain situations
where it is crucial that you are not blamed.
And this list of situations is possibly endless.

The Blame

The world is bruised
It's dark and blue
It's too painful to touch
It's tired too

It's been cut and burnt
The wounds are raw
Another world would heal it,
I'm sure

The world will bite
It's red and dark
It's gnawed away at life,
so sharp

You've been ripped apart
You've been red and blue
But some will always,
lay the blame on you

The Fine Line

There's a fine line between sanity and insanity
A fine line between the past and the present
A fine line between the present and the future
There always
A fine line

A fine line between darkness and dusk
But I know myself more when it's dark
On your deck, I will shine as I steer your sail
Think of us sailing away

I will drive my desire, but it often drives me
And I've never yet known where I've been
There's a fine line between our self-recognition
Our journey – it longs to be free

There's a fine line between the day and the dawn
But both of them, it asks for so much
In your heart you have plans, you may just take a chance
But in your head –
the fine line -
is coated with rust

You play safe – because in that, you trust

The D Word

Dressed in various shades of gold,
he sat upon the throne
Piercing eyes -- with a hollow glare –
He was an enemy unknown

Dressed in various frames of mind,
I hoped that he would go
But his hollow glare, gave things away –
And I was never *quite* alone

I come out of this, unscathed each time
Although he waits for me –
The hollow glare, now all too familiar
Will never fail to be –

The devil crawling through my mind
My nightmare and my pain
Who steals my words - I slur - I whisper –
And I feel, I am, to blame

I liken all these shades of gold,
to backdrops for my dreams
Where vivid nightmares cloud my mind
And feed the past – It seems

And so I've had no other choice –
I've come to *know*, the lurking voice -
The deep depression –
The consciousness –
But I know, I'm *not* alone

He will laugh at himself
   He won't laugh at you

He can't laugh at himself
   He *can* laugh with you...

He's wise and empathetic

Too much laughing

If you need laughter in small doses,
then large amounts may just drag you down
Emojis with tears, gushing from the eyes,
will be like a dolled up clown

I'd like to hide 'em, those laughs and those tears,
For they really drag **me** down

What would become of me if I laughed out loud...
At the slightest light-hearted things?
I would lose my mind –
(I think)

I need my laughs to come in waves
I need to laugh at what you say
I never need to laugh **at** you
With you – *yes*! (If you'd like me to?

What is good for you…

Or for him, for her, for all of them?
He didn't listen,
He just found his way

Four Walls

Indoors, I am within
And I am without
I am safe and I am sane
Indoors I am me
And that's important right?

Outdoors, I am fear
And I'm not there
I long for home
Then I shall be free
And that's okay I'm sure

Indoors, I am within
As I am without the crowd
Indoors, I am within
And I am without a life, you say
But this is my life --
I'm not sure I can see it any other way

Outdoors, it is vast
I am a full-stop
I'm not able to help you -
or myself --
Not while I am here

Indoors, I am within
I can talk, and often I will sing
Shame the world can't understand,
or accept us for being
in

Compulsions

It's got a hold, a tight grip
It forces her to count -
and count -
and count
If anything distracts her,
she'll start again
Tapping the walls on her way down the staircase
Tapping them on the climb back up
Tapping -
counting

-- And then there's the kitchen -
A zone of rules and dirt
The crumbs that fall -
She must never buy bread again

And the car at the crossing -
Someone lying face down
An injury caused by her
But you remind her it wasn't -
"Drive home now, drive home"
-- Rest on the bed -
Radio on -
Music distracts -
And this day is gone, you have won

Tomorrow she knows,
she'll be scrubbing the driveway,
gloves on her hands
Bleach on the ground -
Then after four hours, she'll go back to the house

Tonight on her mind ---
What did she need?
What must she buy?
Where are the lists?

She will dust them today

Locked into a world with the tightest of grips
The energy holds her -
It is never her fault

It is never that easy -
to be confined ---
to be locked

Can you let go?

Without any expectations from yourself,
and certainly not from others…

There is a chance you *can* let go
Maybe not now
Maybe not next month
And maybe you won't exactly know…

How or when *you let go*

Non Attachment

Let go of the puzzle, let go
Throw every piece to the wind
Lay yourself in a bath, on a rug, or on grass
Let your mind go astray, let it go

Let go of that place, let go
It's no longer a part of your world
Sit here with someone, pull up a chair
Let it go, it is done – let it go

Let go of the words, let 'em go
Shout each one out, for the air
Allow yourself time,
Let go of the pain
Let go of your desire to care --

For it is done, for it's done –
Let it go

Bulimia Bites

He was talking to a mate on the landline
And dipping his hand in and out of a box of cereal
I was emptying his fridge, one tomato and limp lettuce
leaves
And then checking the date on the milk

Eating and listening was he
Eating endlessly
Relentlessly –
He was happier to be listening, not talking
I thought about giving him a hug
For I certainly was taken aback
by his endless endless eating
The unhappy snack

I hadn't known him that long
I dropped some lettuce onto the tiles
The dog turned his nose up
And that made him smile

The rigid packet and the cereal crunch
The bellow of the box –
It was time for lunch
He smiled at my obvious concern,
placed the receiver back where it belonged –
And climbed the stairs to be sick

He was sick, *so* sick that it broke my heart
I called him softly --
"You've noticed that my bodies not mine" he said
"And thanks for tidying the fridge"

Cereal crumbling - my stomach turning
I had no idea he lived like this
And I've no idea why

"I'm fine" he says. *"I just cannot be a sensible eater"*
And then I spotted more lettuce on the floor
Hunger, full – diet coke
Stuffed, but empty – no control
Salad cream, salad – fading away
Working it off – vomit today
Vomit tomorrow – lie in shame
Diet coke – jugs of water
Ice, more water
Juice and crisps – potato chips
No one knows his pain –
his shame –
his diary –
his hell –
He has a story in him, but never tell, never tell
Bulimia burning the inside of his throat

Cereal boxes and crumbling toast

The first time she heard a voice inside her head,
she thought it was a friend…

A new friend, that she'd never yet met

And he sounded like a newsreader,
gentle and matter of fact
She takes him most places,
and if she didn't…
then he'd sure invite himself

The People Who Make Us Laugh

Trapped inside a jam jar
But *with* a sense of humour
She will climb out of windows just to make you smile
But she's trapped inside depression
The gift of humour is no surprise ---

Why is someone funny? – they can't possibly be depressed
(But this question is frustrating I confess)
Trapped inside a jam jar, no light and no way out
But she says such funny things – that I'd hate to be without
How can someone be so funny, and at the same time so depressed?
One short answer coming,
they was never meant to be a link ---
Funny people, trapped inside their hell, and if you think ---
Of what could be looming over them –
Or what may keep walking in their way –
You'd expect to always find them laughing –
They are just people, funny people
I hope they'll always stay

It's the confusion of a personality disorder
that leads to misunderstanding

It could well be caused by
genetic and brain chemistry or the past…
such as childhood needs that were never met

Knowing someone with a personality disorder
shouldn't be a shock

The Disorder

Curled up on the sofa, blanket pulled towards my chin
Eyes closed
I shiver, for I feel cold

Out there, you are cleaning cars
walking dogs and crossing roads

Curled up til I decide to watch tv,
Eyes open, Eyes closed
Soup for tea

I loved you, but I loved you too quickly
But I'm where I need to be
And if I sleep tonight, it'll be because I need to make
that great escape from *me*

Wandering the bedroom, and looking lost I know
I bear the cockerel in the background
and the magpie to and fro
I look for shoes, and grab my coat
I'll leave them in the hall
Watch tv, eat the soup, then it's *you* who I will call

I'm fine -- I'm not -- I am again
I'm always fine for you
I was okay until I sank
In my exhausting --
'nothing new'

The Ability To Heal

Bandage my wound until all I have left,
Is the scar
I'll be proud of the process in which I can heal,
Until all I have left is the scar
I will check my wound daily, add ointment and cream
Give it time to be exposed to the air –
I will handle myself with much care

Rebandage the wound until all I have left,
is the need to dispose of the cause
It will always be visible, as will the scar
But *never* will it be what it was

I will touch my own heart, feel it beat through the wound
And I will know what I once failed to perceive
I am wiser, calmer, still methodical though –
And this I believe – is the *'me'*

Bandage my wound until all I have left,
Is the scar
I'll be proud of the process in which I can heal,
Until all I have left is the scar
I will check my wound daily, add ointment and cream
Give it time to be exposed to the air –
I will handle myself with much care –
And believe in myself – in the *'me'*

No Time To Think

Here I go, on the rollercoaster, nothing can hold me back
I'm high as whatever, with no time to describe it –
and I've barely, no time to think
Ideas collide, they pierce my mind –
No way could I ever ignore!
Here I go, are you ready to keep up the pace?
Are you ready or aren't you quite sure?

I can take on the world, so grab your coat, and your phone
Off we go to 'this world' (I'm excited you know)!
Ideas collide, they are great while they last –
Grab your coat, off we go – For these thoughts never last

They are high, like whatever! – too high to be deep
And when I tumble, I end up in a dungeon too steep
A canyon, a dark place, a trap deep within
I'm aware that my sinking will pull me right in

There I go, see you there – see my weary day long
And the eve of whatever I will have to bring on
The high is profound – but the high that comes down
Drags me under the ground –
Here I go – Somehow, I will just carry on
Here I go – Just watch me, move on

I have lost the natural ability to sleep
Hour by hour, I have lost the chance…
And what good does it do to count sheep
Or to count the hours that pass

Another Night Awake

*My legs are nervously moving non-stop. Tight, tense -
It would be almost unnoticeable, but I am the movement of my legs
And now, I am the tension of my hands
How I'd like life to have been of late - *this* is on my mind
Mistakes I've made, and how I felt - this *too* is on my mind
I am the bearer of my fears, and of my life that slips on by
I am wide awake, alert - So restless are my nights
My body is responding to my uneasy mind
Hollow thoughts - I cannot distinguish between,
the day - today - tonight
*It's dark for now - I know my mind is racing to the door
My body restless - my breathing fast - I get out of bed --
I *too* - reach for the door
Sleep eludes me - Life disturbs me - Sleep I cannot find it
I pace the floor, along the hallway - No peace within my mind
* nothings resting in my head, I hear voices out of tune
I go back to bed - My legs are tired – And finally, they rest -
I pull the sheet towards my head, I know how I used to asleep
But *me* in my life wears me out, something somewhere, lets me down
*Tight, tense - recognisable, the past - and the here - and the now
Life consumes me late at night - I cannot drift away
If I *do* - drift away - Or I manage to dream away --
Will those faces come to me?
Or will I see familiar faces, just before I fall asleep?
If I do - I will escape - but not before the morn
Hollow thoughts would then become -
Vivid, full - but torn

So closing my eyes – well it's the best I can do

My kitchen is an uncomfortable place
I fear the food I prepare –
And I fear it may harm you…
There is so much bacteria out there
And so much dirt

The Kitchen Panic

I can be as careful as possible but one splash will occur
That is why I can't cook tomatoes
Various cleaning fluids
Vigorous cleaning fluids
My kitchen is full
Not enough space for food
Once I've cleaned every inch of the bench –
I repeat the process –
And then I repeat it again
No form of bleach is strong enough,
And soap for my hands, is good enough
No towel, no cloth –
Nothing the world has got ---
lives up to the test

My kitchen shall not be a mess –
For I will use it less –
And the more I get used to eating non-messy food,
the happier I will become
I need to get this right –
As my cooking days have come to an end
My cooking days are done!

Be The Therapy

Trauma therapy for me, is building with lego
I spend hours creating a safe place
Or hours recreating my footsteps - my past
Trauma therapy for me is watching dramas on tv
I'm selective, I chose wisely
And I become *lost* in the skill of the role of the editor –
Or of the director --
And the writer and actors --
The dress and the scenes – I admire it all –
They work so well for me

My flashbacks are gruesome, unbearable and real
I loathe their desire to come back *to me* –
To urge me to *feel* them, deep on my hands
Deep as they tear my flesh and my mind
Post trauma, engulfs me –
I have seen it at night –
where *time* can't distract me –
I need to sleep, not fight
I don't need to see faces of the family I knew –
Or the hurt they created, and those trumpets they blew
Lego today – I am building a park
And maybe one evening – I will *build* after dark

You Can Do This
(Even If It's One Day Here And There)

I saw a spider web across my pathway,
As newly spun as the day
I heard the raindrop faint was it's sound,
Upon my window pane
I had woken too early, I will not cope today –
But what I will do, and always have done –
Is let my mind go astray
No pressure, it's Sunday and it's a day off from stress
No pressure on myself, I'll do all that I can –
No stress!
And when I lay down for the night,
I will look through a gap –
In my curtains of blue – onto a night sheer black
I am positive today, although I'm as tired as hell
Make the most of it – I tell myself –
So I spent my time well

I used to keep dandelion clocks, in a box
A dark brown wood, and a golden hinge
They waited for me until I was ready
Their time came…
to be released

Once they were free… So was I

No Expectations

Weep and let go -
If you can

Do one or the other -
If you can't do both?

If you can't do *either* -
Then just go with the flow

Be who you are -
In the way that you know

But believe, (if you can)
that fragments *will* show
They will leave you, at some point

And in part -

You've let go

As for the weeping
Only you know
And even that's not a given -
But I certainly hope,
at some point -
You *can* let it all *go*

Comforting The Emptiness

A sketch pad of numbness
Distant outlines of the past
The faintest of my memories,
resting in my heart

I seem to unwrite every word
as there's nothing left to say.

I'm burdened by my numbness
So the sketchpad is now closed
Will I ever draw another twist
to a plot I can't unfold?

Will I ever see another moment
on any given day,
where I will need the winter air
…to wrap me up and stay.

Built On Pressure

A dysfunctional place is this world
Layer by layer, built by our hands -
And built by our minds – -
Absurd

Deviously wicked is this world
Where our minds absurd –
Just turn every corner, and walk every line –
To be heard

All we have built on
Is *our* expectations --
Some allegations,
and even more -- accusations

Never learning - but cursing
A need and a longing -
And doing whatever, we may need to do

And all the damn time,
Life keeps on pushing –
And there is constant pressure –
That is pointing at *you*

But some of us are learning –
And refusing to 'give in' –
And doing whatever –
we are able to do

I don't even recognise my anxiety
It's been with me for so long…

Anxiety Passing

Something is watching over me
I'm yet to find out who
It has a silhouette
that moves across the room.

It sees my broken body,
and the anxiety in my head
It's getting close to 4 am
I'm desperate for some rest

He takes me to a sacred place
I'm connecting with his mind
He lays me down and covers me
He keeps me safe in sight

Anxiety will harm me
and turn me into someone else
But whatever silhouette did linger
It laid me down to rest

Thank You For Reading

If you decide you have no further use
for this book, Please could you
kindly pass it on to someone else,
Who you think may benefit
from reading it

Thank You

Biography:

I was born in South Wales in 1967.
My family background has mixed heritage, and within this,
I mostly feel that I identify with Wales (Cymru)
and Italy (Italia)
I spent a lot of time, and have a lot of,
wonderful childhood memories of
both the West of Wales and Cornwall (Kernow)
I'm also a spare time artist who admires art in general.
I have always been a quiet person,
and more interested in natural environments
than in city life, and maybe that is because I am quiet.
It enables me to think and feel at ease in such a chaotic world.
But who knows!
All I know is that poetry has helped me find myself
almost fully. And I say *almost*, because I'm not sure
we ever stop finding ourselves in one way or another.
Together with my writing,
my passion for music, art, wildlife,
and poetry in general, I'm more able to understand,
and accept, who I truly am.

Printed in Great Britain
by Amazon